SUPER HAPPY PARTY BEARS

THE

JITTERBUG

THE JITTERBUG

MARCIE COLLEEN

[Imprint]
MAKE YOUR MARK
NEW YORK

A part of Macmillan Children's Publishing Group,
a division of Macmillan Publishing Group, LLC
175 Fifth Avenue, New York, N.Y. 10010

Library of Congress Control Number: 2016954109
ISBN 978-1-250-11359-7 (paperback) / ISBN 978-1-250-11358-0 (ebook)
Our books may be purchased in bulk for promotional, educational, or
business use. Please contact your local bookseller or the Macmillan
Corporate and Premium Sales Department at (800) 221-7945 ext. 5442
or by e-mail at MacmillanSpecialMarkets@macmillan.com.

Book design by Christine Kell
Imprint logo designed by Amanda Spielman
Illustrations by Steve James

First Edition—2017

1 3 5 7 9 10 8 6 4 2

mackids.com

FOR CHRIS,
WHO GOT HER WINGS

CHAPTER ONE

Welcome to the Grumpy Woods!

Actually, if you know what's good for you, you might want to tiptoe out of here. *Very quietly.*

Everyone here is extremely cranky.

It's gotten even worse ever since

1

Flying Blind, the bat-only punk rock band, set up an all-night concert on the Grumpy Flats and kept the townscritters awake way past their bedtime. Luckily, the Super Happy Party Band joined in with a few verses of "If You're Happy and You Know It," which changed

2

the sound of the music and sent
all the Flying Blind fans, and the
band itself, packing. So I guess you
can say the bears saved the day.
Of course, don't give credit to the
Super Happy Party Bears in front of
Mayor Quill unless you want to be
caught up in a quill storm. And his

quills have just grown back after several outbursts.

Once rid of midnight concerts, the townscritters of the Grumpy Woods slept and slept and slept and slept. Right now you are probably thinking *Sleeping for a long time was just what they needed* and *The townscritters must have felt so rested.* Well, no. The crazy thing is, they were groggy and even grumpier than before! Apparently, they slept *too* much.

When they woke up, Humphrey Hedgehog, assistant deputy to Mayor Quill, was excited about a

dream he had regarding a way to
keep bands from performing in the
Grumpy Woods. He drafted some
blueprints and then insisted that
Mayor Quill hold a very official
meeting at City Hall.

Everyone, from Squirrelly Sam

to Dawn Fawn, attended. Except
the Super Happy Party Bears. They
weren't invited because, well, they
are too happy. Humphrey was
cranky from too much sleep and
didn't want to be around anyone
who was cheery and might distract

the townscritters from the topic at hand.

"An open field just asks for trouble," proclaimed Humphrey, unrolling his blueprint. "I propose we cover the Grumpy Flats with thorny berry bushes and rename it the Grumpy Bramble."

"Like blueberry bushes?" asked Mayor Quill.

"No. I want to use berries that grow on bushes with thorns. Like raspberries," explained Humphrey.

"Like sssstrawberriessss?" asked Sheriff Sherry.

"No. Those don't have thorns. But like blackberries," said Humphrey.

"Like bananas?" asked Bernice Bunny.

"Like coconuts?" asked Squirrelly Sam.

"No!" yelled Humphrey.

Mayor Quill was deep in thought. His brow was scrunched. He didn't look too happy with Humphrey's plan.

Finally, he spoke up. "I have a better idea. I propose we cover the Grumpy Flats with thorny boysenberry bushes, and some raspberry and blackberry ones,

and rename it the Grumpy
Bramble."

"Now, that's an interesting
thought," said Squirrelly Sam.

"Let's put it to a vote," said
Bernice.

They did, and Mayor Quill's
proposal won in a landslide victory
over Humphrey's. That was that.

It was very official. The gardening project started immediately.

And so, lately, everyone in the Grumpy Woods wakes up covered from head to toe with thorn scratches and orders up some breakfast—two fresh-from-the-oven eye rolls served with a pat of butter and a few slices of *Baloney!*

That is, everyone except the Super Happy Party Bears.

If you travel just beyond the new Grumpy Flats, which is now the new Grumpy Bramble (you have to keep up here!), and follow the carefully placed sticks, laid out in the shape of arrows, up the flower-lined path, you'll see a welcome sign. That's the Party

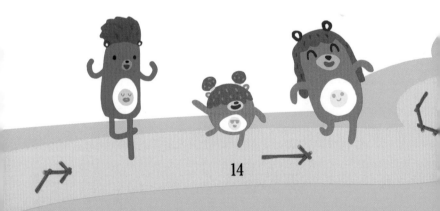

Patch, the Headquarters of Fun.

Life there is very different.

LIFE IS SUPER.

Life is happy. Life is full of parties!

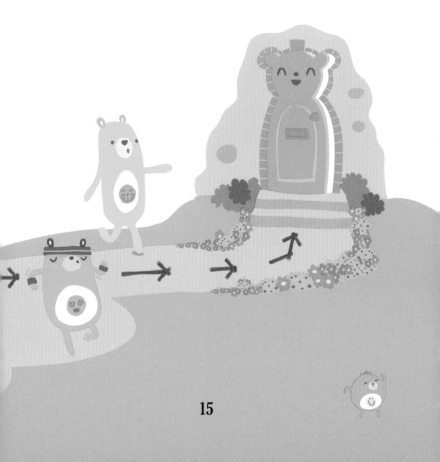

And so, every morning, the
Super Happy Party Bears wake
up ready to tackle the day and
order up some breakfast—a
toppling tower of slaphappy cakes
garnished with a spoonful of
Peachy keen!

Nothing annoys the critters of the Grumpy Woods more.

Except when the bears have a party.

And they are always having a party.

CHAPTER TWO

It was berry season in the Grumpy
Woods. Or, as the Super Happy
Party Bears liked to call it, jelly
doughnut season! Sure, the
Grumpy Bramble was difficult
to harvest. Its thorny mesh
of raspberry, blackberry, and

boysenberry bushes formed a
tightly knit hedge to keep out any
and all bears. But the bears simply
donned their Hug-a-Mayor suits.
After all, they never got close
enough to Mayor Quill to use the
twig-and-pinecone armor before he

Mayoral
Decree
24.600
The mayor does
NOT hug anyone,
ever!
Mayor Quill

decreed *The mayor does not hug
anyone, ever!* He even underlined
it not once, not twice, but five
times. No one dared argue with
that.

So, the Hug-a-Mayor suits were
paired with some newly whittled

stilts for bramble-berry picking. It worked splendidly.

The bears, with juice-stained paws and faces, hauled basket after basket of berries to the Party Patch.

It was time for the daily doughnut preparation.

All the berries were dumped into a blow-up swimming pool in the center of the dance floor.

Big Puff hit his drumsticks together. "ONE, TWO, THREE, FOUR!"

The Super Happy Party Band jammed out some berry-squashing tunes as two bears smashed and mashed, squishing the berries as they danced inside the pool.

"Jelly making is slippery!" The littlest bear giggled as he slid and almost fell.

"Jam is like happiness," said Bubs, calmly blowing party-perfect bubbles

23

over the berries. "You can't spread even a little without getting some on yourself."

Just then, there was a knock on the Party Patch door.

"ONE! TWO! THREE! WHO CAN IT BEEEEEEEEEEE?" sang out the bears.

Now, normally a dozen pairs of furry feet would shuffle over to the door to greet the visitors. However, the bears' feet were a bit busy— and sticky—at the moment.

KNOCK! KNOCK! KNOCK!

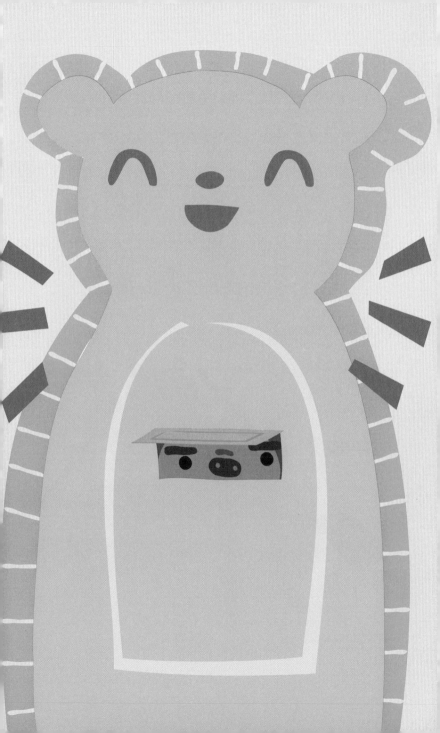

Whoever was on the other side of the door was growing impatient.

Thinking fast, Tunes and Jacks each grabbed a stilt and rowed the jelly-filled pool across the room while the band played "Row, Row, Row Your Pool."

Once at the door, they sang

out again, "ONE! TWO! THREE!
WHO CAN IT BEEEEEEEEEEE?"
The bears swung the door open
wide just as Humphrey Hedgehog
reached up to knock a fourth time,
instead knocking on the purple
one's nose, which caused him to
sneeze right in Humphrey's and
Sherry's faces.

"VISITORS!" cheered the bears.

Humphrey pulled out a
hankie and wiped himself dry.

"Hop aboard," said Tunes.

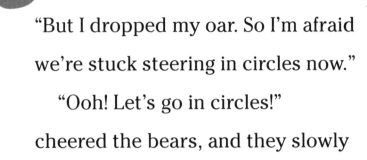

"But I dropped my oar. So I'm afraid
we're stuck steering in circles now."

"Ooh! Let's go in circles!"

cheered the bears, and they slowly

started to spin the jelly-filled

pool with one stilt.

"Enough!" said Humphrey.

"We are here on very official

business. By order of Mayoral Decree number two four six oh one: If a loaf of bread does not belong to you, you have no right to eat it!"

Mayoral
Decree
24.601

If a loaf of bread does not belong to you, you have no right to eat it!

Mayor Quill

"Thissss morning Mayor Quill ssssat down for hissss breakfasssst and found only crumbssss where hissss toasssst had been," explained Sherry.

"Sam was in the branches above City Hall at the time and said he saw a flash of green and pink dance out of the building and head toward the Party Patch," said Humphrey.

Sherry and Humphrey eyed Mops and Jacks and their

berry-stained paws. "We've caught you red-handed. And red-footed. And red-faced," Humphrey added.

"Everyone out of the pool," said Sherry.

But before Sherry could get out her handcuffs (not an easy task without hands),

a green caterpillar with a tuft of
pink fuzzy hair Hula-Hooped a
doughnut past the bears in their
jelly-filled pool and the two

accusing townscritters. When the caterpillar, who was humming a happy little tune, noticed that he was being watched, he paused on the flower-lined path and devoured the doughnut in one bite, leaving only a few crumbs.

"Ta-da!" the caterpillar sang, and waved six jazz hands in the air.

CHAPTER THREE

"He's adorable!" cheered the
bears.

Humphrey crouched down
to get a better look at the green
caterpillar with the pink hair atop
his head and realized that this was
probably the green-and-pink culprit

Sam had witnessed leaving City Hall. "By Mayoral Decree number two four six oh one—"

The caterpillar just giggled and started to do the chicken dance. The bears quickly joined in.

"Enough!" said Humphrey. "This

caterpillar *stole* the mayor's toast and one of your doughnuts. We do not tolerate thievery in the Grumpy Woods."

"Doughnut sharing is doughnut caring," said Bubs.

"Were you hungry, little guy?" asked Jacks.

The caterpillar's eyes grew big and watery as he nodded in reply.

"You sssshould have asssked, then," Sherry scolded.

The caterpillar shimmied over to snuggle Sherry and scooted up to her neck. He flashed a smile at his reflection in her badge.

"Do you know this creature?" Humphrey asked Sherry. "You do look a lot alike."

Sherry shrugged the caterpillar off and hissed at Humphrey.

"What's your name, little guy?" asked the littlest bear.

The caterpillar started to break-dance. He popped to the left. He stomped to the right. Roll, roll, robot arms. Then he wriggled across the path like a worm, spun on his head, and balanced on one hand as he bounced in circles. He finished off with jazz hands and a "Ta-da!" The bears saw that he had written the

word BUTTER in the dirt.

"Welcome to the Party Patch, Butter!" said Mops.

The bears applauded.

"IT'S SUPER HAPPY BUTTER TIME! SUPER HAPPY BUTTER TIME!" they all chanted, and did their Super Happy Party Dance. Butter joined in.

 Slide to the right.

 Hop to the left.

Shimmy, shimmy,
shake.

Jazz hands. "Ta-da!"

Butter rubbed up against the littlest bear's legs like a cat and licked at the drying berry juice.

"Can we keep him?" asked the littlest bear.

"A pet is a big responsibility," said Humphrey.

"WE LOVE RESPONSIBILITY!" cheered the bears.

"Well, in that case," said
Humphrey, "you are to report to
City Hall immediately to register
your animal. And I hereby give you
this ticket for improper pet control.
Make sure he doesn't steal any
more food. The mayor requires
his morning toast with butter."

Butter perked up at his name.

"Not you," said Humphrey.

Humphrey slapped the ticket into Ziggy's paw.

"What is this?" asked Ziggy.

"A fine," said Humphrey.

"A fine what?" asked Ziggy.

"Not a fine *what*," said Humphrey. "Just a fine."

Little Puff dashed into the Party Patch and scribbled with her crayons on some paper. She came back and slapped the paper into the hedgehog's paw. It was a drawing of Humphrey.

"We think you are fine, too, Humphrey," she said.

"GROUP HUG!" cheered the bears.

"Ack!" screamed Humphrey, turning quickly to avoid the group hug. But before he could escape, he smacked right into the Party Patch

welcome sign, dislodging a few of
the stick-figure townscritters from
the diorama sitting on top.

The stick figure of Mayor Quill
bounced off Sherry's head and
bonked Humphrey on the nose.

"Pardon me, sir," Humphrey
called back to the wooden

porcupine as he hurried down the
path with Sherry on his heels.

"Humphrey never says good-bye,"
Bubs explained to Butter. "Because
saying good-bye means being away
from the ones he loves."

CHAPTER FOUR

The bears finished up their batch
of special Grumpy Bramble berry
doughnuts. Butter loved the warm
pillows of dough bursting with
fresh jam. Jacks lost track of just
how many doughnuts Butter ate.

But it was around a dozen. For a

little guy, he sure could eat a lot!

To clean up, they filled the now-

empty blow-up pool with sudsy

water perfect for a bath.

"POOL PARTY!" they cheered

as, one by one, they cannonballed

into the bubbles. Butter joined in, holding on to the stick-figure Mayor Quill as a floaty.

Once squeaky-clean, they headed down to City Hall to get Butter registered, as Humphrey had instructed.

They all paraded out of the Party
Patch, down the flower-lined path,
and straight to City Hall. Butter rode
along on the littlest bear's shoulder
like a pirate's parrot. However,
instead of squawking or saying
"Aarghh" like a pirate, Butter kept
striking poses and saying "Ta-da!"
Which caused the bears to also
strike poses and say "Ta-da!" It took
a very long time to get to City Hall.

Mayor Quill, as usual, was not in the mood for dancing. His whole morning had been filled with complaints from townscritters.

Apparently, Butter had been eating his way around the Grumpy Woods.

"My clover patch was mowed down to nothing," said Bernice. "Even my specialty four-leaf variety."

"WhoOOOo dared steal my tea leaves?" screeched Opal.

"My vegetablessss were all harvessssted!" complained Sherry.

"Now, see, you didn't strike me as the vegetable-patch type," said Humphrey to Sherry.

"I'm a garden ssssnake,"

explained Sherry. "It helpssss me with sssstresssss."

"You didn't hear this from me," said Sam, "but we're all going to starve!"

"GRUMBLY TUMMY! GRUMBLY TUMMY! GRUMBLY TUMMY!" sang Dawn Fawn.

As Dawn sang, the bears and
Butter shuffled through the door.

"Ooh! WE LOVE PARTIES!"
exclaimed the bears upon seeing all
their neighbors.

Jigs glanced around the room. "If
this is a party, where's the food?"
she whispered loudly to Ziggy.

The townscritters scowled.

Mayor Quill quivered. A quill storm was brewing.

"Nice of you to join us," he said through clenched teeth. "I see you have brought your *pet*."

"This is Butter," said the littlest bear. He motioned to his shoulder, but Butter wasn't there.

Butter was on Mayor Quill's desk, munching on some papers. When Butter realized that everyone was watching him, he moonwalked across a pile of books, did a quick pirouette, and then waved his six jazz hands. "Ta-da!"

The bears applauded. "Isn't he the cutest?"

60

Mayor Quill shook with anger but calmly took his empty breakfast bowl, turned it upside down, and trapped Butter underneath.

"By order of Mayoral Decree number two four six oh one," the mayor yelled to the overturned bowl, "if a loaf of bread does not belong to you, you have no right to eat it! Additionally, by order of Mayoral Decree number two four six oh one point ONE, if a patch of clover does not belong to you, you have no right to eat it! Number two four six oh one point TWO, if tea leaves do not belong to you, you have no right to eat them! Number two—"

Humphrey interrupted. "Sir, perhaps we can just say that eating food that is not yours is wrong."

Mayor Quill grumbled and rewrote the decrees with a fresh quill from his belly.

Then, looking at the bears, he

said, "As Humphrey has informed

you, all pets in the Grumpy Woods

must be licensed and properly

controlled. Therefore, I hereby

declare a leash law." He pulled

a leash and collar from his desk

drawer and handed it to the

littlest bear.

"Oooh! WE LOVE ACCESSORIES!"

cheered the bears.

"I can put some sparkles on that," said Shades, "and it will really bling!"

The bears rescued Butter from under the bowl and placed the collar around his small green neck.

Butter simply slipped right out of the collar to get one last chomp of paper.

Mayor Quill couldn't contain his anger any longer. He stomped his foot. He shook from head to toe. Just before he exploded, the townscritters took cover.

Quills ricocheted everywhere.

Three soared straight toward Butter,

who caught them in his hands. And

then, holding the quills like canes,

Butter started to tap-dance.

"Ta-da, sir!" said Humphrey.

CHAPTER FIVE

Back at the Party Patch, it was time for the Super Happy Pet Training to begin. After all, the bears had promised the mayor they would teach Butter how to be polite and behave properly. It had been decreed.

The bears sat in a big circle on the floor and placed Butter in the middle.

"We're going to teach you EVERYTHING we know!" said the littlest bear.

Butter nodded eagerly.

"First thing: doughnuts!" said Little Puff.

"Trust me, Butter knows all about doughnuts," said Jacks.

Butter rubbed his tummy and licked his lips. He made the shape of a doughnut with his long body and rolled around in the center of the circle. The bears applauded and awarded him with a doughnut for a lesson well done.

"Next lesson: dancing!" said Mops, spinning on his head.

Butter brushed the doughnut crumbs off his hands and scampered to the very center of the circle. He gestured to Flips and cleared his throat. Flips, on cue, shined a flashlight through his party hat for a spotlight on Butter.

The little critter snapped his
fingers at Tunes, who pressed PLAY
on her boom box. Butter began to
dance.

Jazz hands. Bounce, bounce.
Step clap. Step clap. Spin. Quick
stop. Duckwalk. "Ta-da!"

The bears cheered.

"Maybe we should be asking this jitterbug to teach us hepcats how to dance," said Big Puff.

"Butter is *already* a Super Happy Party Caterpillar!" cheered the bears.

"I believe our *responsibility* here is done," said Shades, standing up to leave the circle.

Just then, there was a knock on the Party Patch door.

"ONE! TWO! THREE! WHO CAN IT BEEEEEEEEEEEE?" sang out the bears as they scurried over to swing the door open wide, revealing Bernice Bunny. She was holding a large stack of books.

"Fluffy Bottom!" they all cheered.

And before Bernice could object to the nickname she really

despised, she was pulled into the

Party Patch and a cup of juice was

put in her paw.

"Actually, I am only here because Mayor Quill asked me to pull a few books about pet ownership for you from my library," she explained. Her little nose twitched to investigate the contents of the cup she was holding, and she handed it off to Mops.

"We're good. Butter can dance and eat doughnuts! Responsibility done!" said Jacks.

"Being *responsible* for a pet goes way beyond treats and playtime." Bernice squinted at Jacks over her still-twitching nose. "For example," she said, flipping through one of her large books, "it says here that pets need a protected and clean living environment."

Bernice glanced at the pots and pans lying haphazardly everywhere, the scattering of crumbs on the floor, and the splatters of batter on the walls. Party hats and musical instruments were strewn about. A heap of

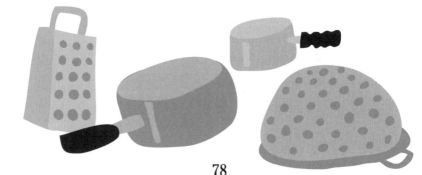

broken piñatas from an earlier
fiesta littered a corner.

She continued. "It also says not
to overlook grooming, as well as
dental care."

Butter grinned generously,
showing off his gleaming chompers.

"You must also train your pet to follow simple commands."

"That one's easy. Watch this," said Big Puff. "Five, six, seven, eight!" Butter immediately started dancing.

Bernice just rolled her eyes.

"I will leave these books with you." She hopped toward the door. "Oh, and make sure he has a quality diet," she said, noticing the lollipop Shades was handing Butter for a dance well done. It was bigger than Butter's head.

Butter took a giant lick and
winked at Bernice. She harrumphed
and hopped out the door, doughnut
crumbs stuck to her little cottontail.

CHAPTER SIX

The bears decided it was much easier to take Butter out for exercise than to clean up the Party Patch, so they headed out to stroll in the Grumpy Woods.

Shades had BeDazzled Butter's purple leash, and it sparkled in the sunlight. It was almost blinding, so the bears wore their Flying Blind sunglasses. They asked Butter if he would wear the collar just for the walk, since Mayor Quill decreed that pets needed to be on a leash when outside.

But Butter was not happy. He couldn't strut while wearing the

leash. He couldn't moonwalk with the leash. He couldn't even country line dance while on the leash.

And even worse, he could smell all the deliciousness of the woods: spicy leaves, juicy veggies, and fragrant flowers. Butter was, yet again, hungry.

That's when he had an idea.

Stopping in the pathway, Butter started to clap a rhythm. Clap. Clap. Clap. Clap. Now if there is anything that the Super Happy Party Bears cannot resist, it's a good rhythm. Once Butter had the bears' attention and they were clapping along, he enacted his plan.

He slid to the right. Hopped to the left. Shimmied, shimmied, shook. And struck a pose.

"Butter's doing our dance!" cheered the bears. Without missing a beat, they quickly joined in.

"IT'S SUPER HAPPY PARTY TIME! SUPER HAPPY PARTY TIME!" They continued to dance with Butter. It was like a flash mob of happiness smack in the middle of the Grumpy Woods.

Slide to the right.

Hop to the left.

Shimmy. shimmy. shake.

Strike a pose.

But instead of striking a pose, Butter kept on shimmying and shaking—right out of his collar.

The bears didn't notice. They were busy doing what Super Happy

Party Bears do best of all. So, Butter moonwalked away, following his nose to the tasty treats.

Bernice's thicket was secluded and hard to navigate. But not for a tiny caterpillar. Once inside, Butter tried to ask for food (as Sherry had said he should). But with Bernice's

nose stuck in a book, she didn't

notice him. So, Butter tap-danced

into her kitchen and through her

freshly baked carrot cake.

Opal Owl's house was high

in a tree. Butter, however,

was an excellent climber. His

moves were like those of a ninja

ballerina—graceful and stealthy. He was about to ask her if he could have something to eat, but Opal snored away. So, not wanting to wake her, Butter made off with most of the contents of her pantry.

And Mayor Quill's door was tightly shut so he could go about his official duties without being disturbed. Butter simply limboed under the door. He was about to ask the mayor for some of the watermelon on his desk, but Butter didn't want to interrupt any official business. So, with three big chomps, he polished off the melon, including the rind, and limboed back out.

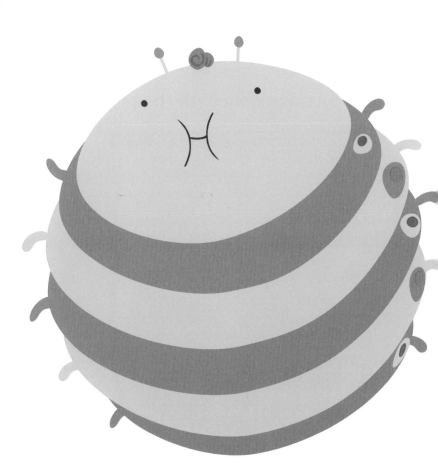

Butter was stuffed. He looked
more like a tennis ball than a long,
slender caterpillar. He slowly crept

back to the pathway, where the Super Happy Party Bears were still dancing. It was a little more difficult to slip into the collar now, but Butter squeezed in.

"Ta-da!" he sang, just barely stretching out six jazz hands.

On cue, the bears struck poses and said, "Ta-da!" That signaled the end of the dance party.

"Butter looks . . . different," said the littlest bear. "Did you do something new with your hair, Butter?"

"Dance can be very transformative," said Bubs.

Butter patted his full belly and let out a huge BUUUUURRRRP!

CHAPTER SEVEN

By the time the bears sashayed

back to the Party Patch, Butter

had worked up another appetite.

His tummy grumbled loudly

enough for everyone to hear.

"Poor little guy," said Jigs. "We

haven't fed him in so long!"

"SNACK TIME!"

cheered the bears. Butter did
a little jig. Snack time was his
favorite of all the times.

The bears formed a parade
of food as, one by one, they
presented Butter with all the
finest—high quality, as Bernice
had specified—foods Party Patch
had to offer: chocolate cake,

ice-cream cones, a pickle with cheese, lollipops, a piece of berry pie, the last jelly doughnut, and one slice of watermelon.

"He's a big guy for a little guy," remarked Shades as Butter gobbled up every last morsel.

"He has the appetite of a champion," said Jacks.

"A very sleepy champion," said Mops.

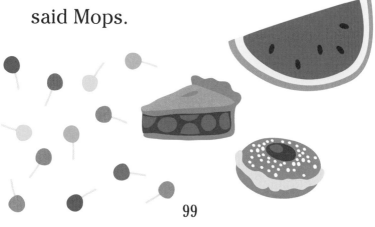

Butter yawned. His eyes
drooped. He could barely stand
up on his many legs. In fact, it
looked like the back half of him had
already fallen asleep.

"NAP TIME!" cheered the bears.

They took off his collar and took great care to create a little nest for Butter. First, they gently placed him on a mountain of their favorite pillows. Next, they piled on all their coziest blankets: quilts,

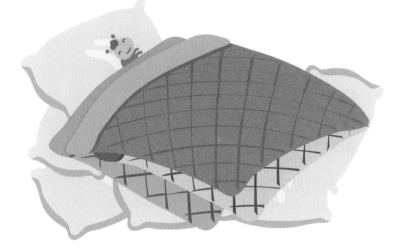

afghans, picnic blankets, and the littlest bear's prized baby blanket on top.

When they were done, they stepped back to admire their handiwork.

"Butter? Where'd you go?" asked Mops.

"Butter!" they called, sifting through the heap.

Finally, they found the caterpillar. He had rolled through gaps between the pillows.

"This is no bed for a caterpillar," said Jigs.

But the bears had never had a slumber party with a caterpillar. None of the beds they created seemed right.

"TOO SMALL."

"TOO BIG."

"TOO SOFT."

"TOO HARD."

Until they found the bed that was just right. It was a perfectly BeDazzled leaf hanging like a hammock from the windowsill.

Butter was lifted onto his bed. Before snuggling up, he nibbled a bit of the leaf. Not only was it cozy, but it was tasty, too. It was perfect!

All the bears gathered around the leaf and sang a lullaby. Butter drifted off to sleep with visions of sugarplums dancing in his head.

"We rock at this responsibility thing," whispered Ziggy.

CHAPTER EIGHT

Butter slept upon his little leaf hammock.

He didn't wake up for the late-afternoon karaoke jam. He didn't move during Jacks's pre-dinner Dancercise Dance-Off. He didn't stir when the bears had their Pajama Relay.

Nope. Butter slept on through. Every so often, the bears would peek at him. They were very proud of how responsible they were being. After all, Bubs had read in one of Bernice's books that "happiness is a sign of a job well done." Butter looked happy. Job well done!

But come morning . . .

Butter was missing! Even his little hammock was gone.

"Where would he go?" asked the littlest bear.

"He didn't leave a note," said Mops.

"And he took his bed with him," said Jacks.

"Maybe he ate it," said Jigs.

"Remember that time Tunes was dreaming about mashed potatoes and ate her pillow?"

Tunes giggled. "I burped feathers for a whole month!"

"We need to form a search party," announced Shades. "Flips, we need your party hat flashlight. Little Puff, draw Butter on some

flyers we can hang up around the Woods. Everyone else, leave no doughnut hole unturned. Take note of anything that could be a clue."

While some of the bears looked low, Jacks decided to look high, with the help of the stilts. It was then that he found a most peculiar clue.

"Where did this tiny piñata come from?" he asked.

Hanging from one of the ceiling rafters was an odd-looking green and sparkly piñata. It glittered in the morning sunlight.

Little Puff sniffled.

"Butter loved piñatas."

"That's it!" said Mops. "I bet
Butter set up the piñata. He

probably wants to throw a fiesta to thank us for everything and is out collecting the other party supplies right now!"

"YAY!" cheered the bears.

"I have an idea," said Jacks. "Let's have a party for Butter when he gets back. It will be a Surprise and Thank-You for the 'Surprise Thank-You Party' Party!"

And just like that, the bears ended their search party and began preparations for a Surprise Thank-You Party. To be a Super Happy

Party Bear, one needs to be able to deftly switch from party theme to party theme.

The Super Happy Party Band tuned up. Ziggy had the perfect song to play once Butter arrived back at the Party Patch. The band started to rehearse.

Big Puff hit his drumsticks together. "ONE, TWO, THREE, FOUR!"

"You put the boom boom into my heart," Ziggy sang.

Just then, there was a BOOM BOOM on the Party Patch door. It was a knock, but an angry-sounding knock.

"ONE! TWO! THREE! WHO CAN IT—?" started the bears, but they were interrupted by Mayor Quill shouting through a megaphone.

"Open up this instant and come

out with all six of your little paws
up!"

The bears raised their paws in
the air and counted. There were
twenty-four paws. Before they
could figure out which six of the
twenty-four Mayor Quill meant,

there was another BOOM BOOM on the Party Patch door. They opened it wide, still sorting out the math problem at hand.

"Where issss he?" asked Sherry.

"Who?" asked Shades.

"That tiny pet of yours who has stolen all our food," explained Humphrey. "Show them, Sam."

Squirrelly Sam was in the tree branches above and unfurled

Stolen Food Items

a lengthy scroll of paper detailing the missing food.

"Butter?" asked Jacks. "He's out getting party supplies for a little fiesta we are having here. He should be back any moment.

Perhaps you can come in and wait for him."

"If Butter is not here, then do you all take responsibility?" asked Mayor Quill.

"Oh, we rock at responsibility!" cheered the bears.

"We've taught Butter everything we know," said the littlest bear.

"In that case," said Mayor Quill into the megaphone, "you are all under arrest for violation of Mayoral Decree number—"

"Wait!" yelled Little Puff over the ruckus. "Quilly, you sound angry. You know what I think would make you feel better? To try our new piñata!"

"YAY!" cheered the bears. They gathered around the townscritters and ushered them into the Party Patch, where Mayor Quill was blindfolded, spun around, and handed a stick. It all happened so quickly he didn't have time to argue.

The odd-looking green and sparkly piñata hung above them all. But before the stick was swung, the piñata began to tremble. It twitched.

"I think the candy wants out,"

the littlest bear said with a giggle.

They all watched as Butter

peeked out of the piñata. "Ta-da!"

CHAPTER NINE

"Butter! That's the best piñata
surprise ever!" cheered the bears.

"This is better than popping out
of a cake," said Shades.

Mayor Quill pulled off his
blindfold and grabbed his

megaphone. "Come down here this instant!" he demanded.

Butter nibbled at the piñata—which wasn't a piñata at all, but a cocoon. He wiggled and squirmed. And then he pushed himself out.

But he didn't look like a Super Happy Party Caterpillar anymore. Nope. He was a beautiful Super Happy Party Butterfly!

He gracefully whisked to and fro through the air.

"Stellar moves, Jitterbug!" said Big Puff.

Butter fluttered to pick up some glitter from a nearby table and then took off again. Like a skywriting plane he flew, leaving a trail of glitter drifting in the air in the shape of a heart.

"Ta-da," he sang. Butter

127

waved his jazz
hands and
headed toward
the window.

"Where's he going?"
asked the littlest bear.

"He's going to get out the
window!" said Tunes.

"We're responsible for you,"
Ziggy called after Butter. "How are
we going to take care of you if you
leave?"

Butter paused on the windowsill.

Mayor Quill put his arm around
Ziggy. "My dear bear, being

responsible is knowing what's best for him."

"A house is no place for a butterfly," added Humphrey. "Butter needs to fly free."

The other townscritters quickly nodded in agreement. Sam scurried and opened every window to make Butter's departure as easy as possible.

"He'll be happy," added Bernice. "You want him to be happy, right?"

Butter waved once again and was about to take flight when the littlest bear called out to him. "Wait! Aren't you forgetting something?"

"It's time for a SUPER HAPPY RE-BIRTHDAY PARTY!" cheered the bears.

The bears
swiftly pulled
together
everything
needed for the
best birthday party ever. All the
townscritters stuck around. They
were so pleased that Butter would
be leaving and their food would be
safe once again that they even
partied a bit themselves. Plus,
the little cannoli made to look like
cocoons were absolutely delicious,
and Humphrey and Sam gobbled
them up.

The Super Happy Party Band played as Butter showed off his new aerial acrobatics. The dance floor moved to the air when the blow-up pool was flipped over and used as a trampoline so everyone could join in the flying. Opal Owl and Butter taught the others how to flip and swoop.

And when Mayor Quill wasn't looking, Tunes and Jacks got a few hugs in, thanks to the Hug-a-Mayor suits.

It was a super party. But soon it was time for good-bye.

Butter kissed each one of the bears on the nose.

The littlest bear giggled. "Butterfly kisses tickle!"

Butter once more grabbed glitter and then took off into the air. Like a skywriting plane he flew, leaving a drifting trail of glitter that spelled out the words THANK YOU.

"We're proud of you, little guy!" said Shades.

"They grow up so fast," said Jacks.

"It's SUPER HAPPY BUTTER TIME! SUPER HAPPY BUTTER TIME!" cheered the bears, and they did their Super Happy Party Dance. And you know what? The townscritters danced, too.

They were feeling just a *little less grumpy*. THE END.

ABOUT THE AUTHOR

In previous chapters, Marcie Colleen has been a teacher, an actress, and a nanny, but now she spends her days writing children's books! She lives in her very own Party Patch, Headquarters of Fun, with her husband and their mischievous sock monkey in San Diego, California. Occasionally, there are even doughnuts. This is her first chapter book series.

Don't Miss the other
SUPER HAPPY PARTY BEARS
Books

GNAWING AROUND

MARCIE COLLEEN

KNOCK KNOCK on WOOD

MARCIE COLLEEN

STAYING A HIVE

MARCIE COLLEEN

GOING NUTS

MARCIE COLLEEN

BAT TO THE BONE

MARCIE COLLEEN

THE JITTERBUG

MARCIE COLLEEN